IMAGINE
YOU and ME

Benson Shum

Dial Books for Young Readers

For all friendships

Randall and Parker looked forward to summers.
Summers meant ice cream.

Discovering new lands.

Visiting magical worlds.

And lifting each other up when needed.

One afternoon, a roar of laughter tumbled their tower.
The laughter was coming from a group of bears playing nearby.

Randall thought they should find another place to play.

Parker didn't agree. She nudged Randall toward the bears.

"What if they don't like me?" asked Randall.

Parker smiled.
She nudged again.

So Randall put on his brave bear face.
"Want to build a castle with us?" asked Randall.

The other bears agreed.

They dug, they carved, they laughed and roared.
Randall wondered, maybe he and Parker
could be a part of this group.
This sloth of bears.

You're so funny Randall!

But there was one problem . . .

. . . they all ignored Parker.

Randall wanted the bears to like Parker.
So he told stories of the time they swam with mermaids.

Explored lost jungles.

Soared through starry skies.

But the bears only saw Randall on a spring rider.

"Who are you talking to?" one asked.
"There's nobody there," said another.

Randall didn't know what to say.
So he stayed quiet.

Then one of the bears invited Randall
to play kickball with them.

Randall wasn't very good at kickball.

So Randall benched himself.
Parker nudged Randall to go out and try again.

"What if I trip and they laugh at me?"

Parker smiled and
nudged again.

Randall wobbled when he kicked the ball.

But the bears were there to catch him.

And the more Randall played with the bears,
the less he played with Parker.

It was just one time, thought Randall.
Parker wouldn't mind.

But on walks, Parker couldn't keep up with the bears.

SCHOOL BUS

And there were no seats left on the bus.

More and more often, Parker just played by herself.

Until one day, Randall realized
he hadn't seen Parker in a while.

Randall looked everywhere.

And the more he looked,

the more Randall felt torn.

Randall was happy to be part of a sloth.
But he missed his friend.
He didn't mean to leave Parker behind.
He hoped Parker was okay.

So Randall decided . . .

. . . to revisit a memory.

As he built the tower higher, Randall started to remember.

He hoped it was enough.

And it was, enough.

As Randall and Parker started a new tower,
one of his friends walked by.

"Can I build a castle with you?" she asked.
"Sure," said Randall.

Then Randall heard a
grumble and a tumble.

The noises were coming from
a little bear playing nearby.

"Want to build a castle with us?" Randall asked.

The little bear agreed.

Randall was suprised—and happy!—to see
that the little bear could see Parker too.

As the sun set, Randall and Parker had to go home. Randall knew Parker had new adventures to find and new friendships to explore.

But their memories together would always be
as vast as the stars and as deep as the sea.

And that was enough.

Dial Books for Young Readers
An imprint of Penguin Random House LLC, New York

First published in the United States of America by Dial Books for Young Readers,
an imprint of Penguin Random House LLC, 2024

Copyright © 2024 by Benson Shum

Visit us online at PenguinRandomHouse.com.

Library of Congress Cataloging-in-Publication Data is available.

Manufactured in China * ISBN 9780593617069 * 10 9 8 7 6 5 4 3 2 1

TOPL

Design by Cerise Steel * Text set in Mali

The art for this book was created using watercolor and ink and compiled in Photoshop.